Ladybird

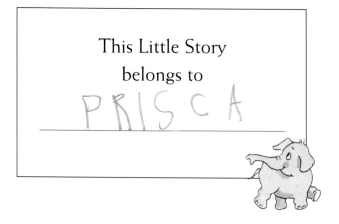

This Little Story
belongs to

PRISCA

A catalogue record for this book is available
from the British Library

Published by Ladybird Books Ltd
A subsidiary of the Penguin Group
A Pearson Company

Illustrations © David Pace MCMXCVII
© LADYBIRD BOOKS LTD MCMXCVII

Brilliant
Little
Elephant

by Joan Stimson
illustrated by David Pace

As soon as she heard the brilliant news, Little Elephant couldn't stop talking about it.

The Head of the Herd had announced the date for the Big Show. And this year Little Elephant was allowed to join in.

Little Elephant skipped round Mum and squealed with excitement.

"You'd better decide what you're going to do," smiled Mum. "And start practising."

Little Elephant set off straightaway in search of ideas.

"Look at me!" cried Little Elephant's cousin from the side of the lake. "I've made some mud balls. And I'm juggling."

Little Elephant watched eagerly.
"That's brilliant!" she squealed.
"Let *me* try." Then she made some
mud balls herself.

But juggling was harder than it looked. One by one the mud balls biffed Little Elephant on the nose.

"OUCH!" she cried. Then she dived into the lake to get clean.

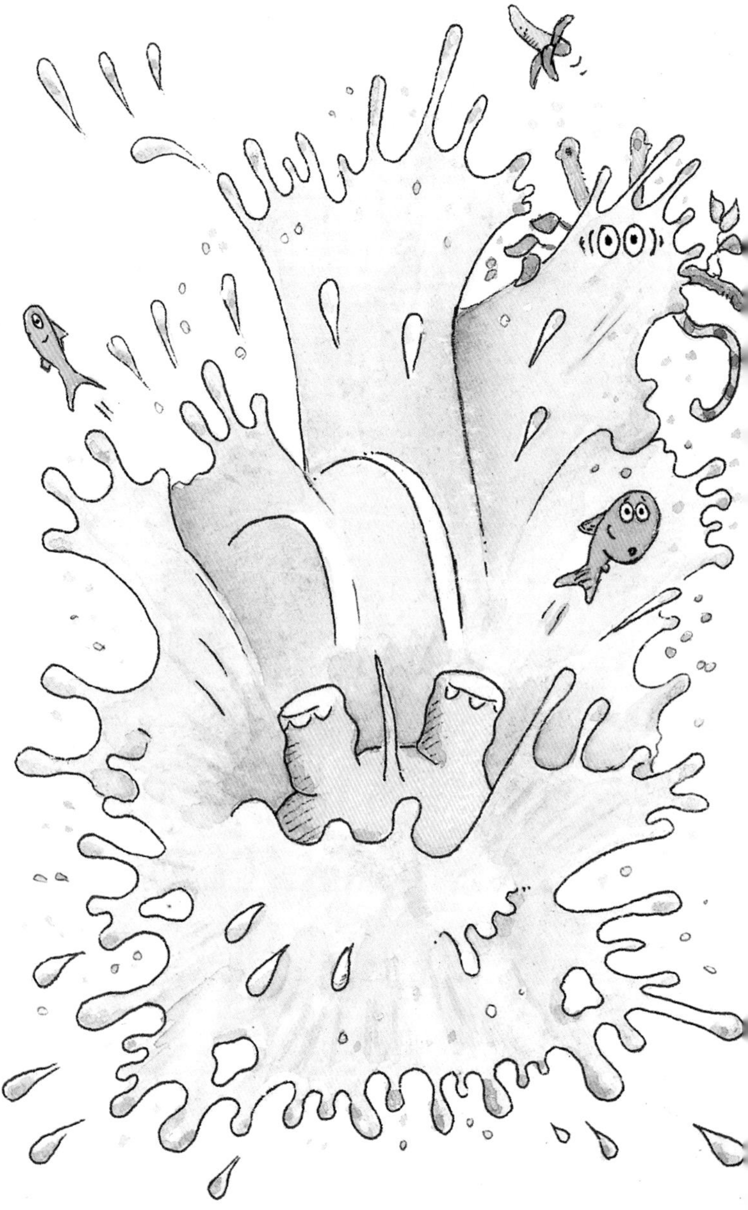

"Look at us!" cried Little Elephant's uncles from the middle of the lake. "We're swimming in time together."

Little Elephant watched eagerly. "That's brilliant!" she squealed. "Let *me* try." Then she splashed across to her uncles.

I'm just a beginner,
But I'll be a winner,
And I'll be the star
Of the show!

But swimming in time was harder than it looked. And soon all the uncles were out of time, too.

"Sorry!" cried Little Elephant. And she swam to the side of the lake to give her uncles some space.

"Look at me!" cried Little Elephant's friend from the bank. "I'm blowing bubbles with my trunk."

Little Elephant watched eagerly. "That's brilliant!" she squealed. Then she dipped *her* trunk in the water. "Let *me* try," she burbled.

But blowing bubbles was harder
than it looked. The water went right
up Little Elephant's trunk. And she
ran sneezing along the shore.

"Look at us!" cried Little Elephant's aunties from a branch overhanging the lake. "We're doing gymnastics."

Little Elephant watched eagerly. "That's brilliant!" she squealed. "Let *me* try." Then she scrambled up beside her aunties…

But, when Little Elephant looked
down, she froze with fright. She
didn't want to do gymnastics after all.

"Never mind, Little Elephant,"
said her aunties. "There must be
something you can do in the show."

But Little Elephant was no longer
sure. And, suddenly, she wanted
her mum.

"Look at me!" cried Mum, as Little Elephant trudged into view. "I'm perfecting my song and dance routine."

Little Elephant listened intently as Mum sang a complicated tune. She looked longingly as Mum's toes twinkled across the grass.

"Why don't you join in, Little Elephant?" said Mum.

But Little Elephant shuffled and shook her head.

"It's too difficult," she wailed. "I've tried out *all* the acts," she explained. "But I can't do *any* of them!"

Little Elephant's mum stopped dancing and began to think.

At last she had a brilliant idea.

"I know what you can do, Little Elephant," she beamed.

And off they went to the Head of
the Herd to arrange it.

On the night of the Big Show the elephants all gathered by the lake.

"I wonder what Little Elephant's going to do?" they whispered to each other.

Then, as the moon rose, Little Elephant herself appeared in the centre of the display area. And, when at last the audience was silent, she squealed with pride.

Well, don't you look great?
And you won't have to wait
For more than a quick 'hello'.
Though I'm a beginner
Each act is a winner...

And we've got a BRILLIANT show!

"HOORAY!" cried all the elephants. "Little Elephant is going to be the PRESENTER!"

And, because talking was what Little Elephant did best, she introduced every single act… BRILLIANTLY!